Another Point of View

The Three Billy Goats Gruff

retold by Dr. Alvin Granowsky
illustrations by Thomas Newbury

STECK-VAUGHN
COMPANY
ELEMENTARY • SECONDARY • ADULT • LIBRARY

Once upon a time, there were three billy goats named Gruff. The littlest billy goat was called Little Billy Goat Gruff. The middle billy goat was called Middle Billy Goat Gruff. The biggest billy goat was called Big Billy Goat Gruff.

These three billy goats lived in a meadow where the grass grew tall and green. But the goats had been chomping on the grass every day since early spring, and most of the tasty blades were gone.

One day, Little Billy Goat Gruff said, "I'm going to the hillside where the grass grows tall and green. Who wants to come with me to eat that yummy-looking grass?"

His bigger brothers looked up at the green hillside. "That grass sure does look good!" his brothers said. "Yes, we'll come, but first we need to do our work. You run along, and we'll meet you up there before too long."

6

"See you up on the hillside!" Little Billy Goat Gruff called. "I promise I won't eat all the yummy grass before you get there!" The little goat started happily on his way.

But the only way to get to the hillside was over a rickety, wooden bridge. A mean, old troll lived under that bridge. The scary troll had eyes that bulged with fire and teeth that were big, sharp, and pointed. And his favorite dinner was goat!

Little Billy Goat Gruff came to the rickety
bridge and began to cross it.

trip-trap trip-trap trip-trap

"Who's that crossing over my bridge?" roared
the mean, old troll in his deep, scary voice.

"It's just me, Little Billy Goat Gruff," the little goat trembled. "I'm going over to the hillside to eat the yummy grass."

"You want to eat the yummy grass!" the mean, old troll roared. "Well, I want to eat the yummy, little you!"

"Oh, please don't eat me!" cried Little Billy Goat Gruff. His legs were shaking so badly, he looked as if he would fall right over. "Wait until Middle Billy Goat Gruff comes. He's much bigger than I am, and he'll be so much more for you to eat!"

"Great!" roared the scary troll. "I would much rather have a larger meal than a smaller one. Trot along over to the hillside, little goat! I'll wait to eat your bigger brother!"

Little Billy Goat Gruff ran for his life as fast as his little hooves would carry him.

trip-trap trip-trap trip-trap

Just a short while later, Middle Billy Goat
Gruff came along and started across the rickety,
wooden bridge.

Trip-Trap Trip-Trap Trip-Trap

"Who's that crossing over my bridge?" roared
the mean, old troll in his deep, scary voice.

"It's just me, Middle Billy Goat Gruff," the middle-sized goat trembled. "I'm going over to the hillside to eat the yummy grass."

"You want to eat the yummy grass!" the mean, old troll roared. "Well, I want to eat the yummy you!"

14

"Oh, please don't eat me!" cried Middle Billy Goat Gruff. His legs were shaking so badly, he looked as if he would fall right over. "Wait until Big Billy Goat Gruff comes. He's much bigger than I am, and he'll be so much more for you to eat!"

"Great!" roared the scary troll. "I would much rather have a big meal than a middle-sized one. Trot along over to the hillside, middle-sized goat! I'll wait to eat your bigger brother!"

Middle Billy Goat Gruff ran as fast as his middle-sized hooves would carry him.

Trip-Trap Trip-Trap Trip-Trap

Just a short time later, Big Billy Goat Gruff came along and started across the rickety, wooden bridge.

TRIP-TRAP TRIP-TRAP TRIP-TRAP

"Who's that crossing over my bridge?" roared the mean, old troll in his deep, scary voice.

"It's just me, Big Billy Goat Gruff!" the big goat said in his loud, clear voice. "I'm going over to the hillside to eat the yummy grass!"

"You want to eat the yummy grass!" the mean, old troll roared. "Well, I want to eat the big, yummy you!"

"You want to eat me, do you?" laughed Big Billy Goat Gruff. He was so big and strong that he wasn't afraid of anyone. He pawed the bridge and lowered his great big horns. "Then come right on over! I'm waiting for you!"

The mean, old troll leaped on top of the bridge. His eyes bulged with fire. His big, sharp, pointed teeth flashed in the sunlight. "Now I've got you!" he roared.

"That's what you think!" replied Big Billy Goat Gruff. Then he charged at the mean, old troll and knocked him high into the air. The troll went over the bridge and fell into the water below. He was never seen again.

Then Big Billy Goat Gruff trotted over the bridge to the green hillside where the tall blades of grass grew.

He smiled at his brothers. "How do you
like it here on the hillside?" he asked.

"Just fine!" the two goats said. "The tall
grass sure is yummy." Then they asked,
"How's that mean, old troll who lives under
the bridge?"

Another Point of View

JUST A FRIENDLY OLD TROLL

by Dr. Alvin Granowsky

illustrations by Michele Nidenoff

STECK-VAUGHN
COMPANY
ELEMENTARY • SECONDARY • ADULT • LIBRARY

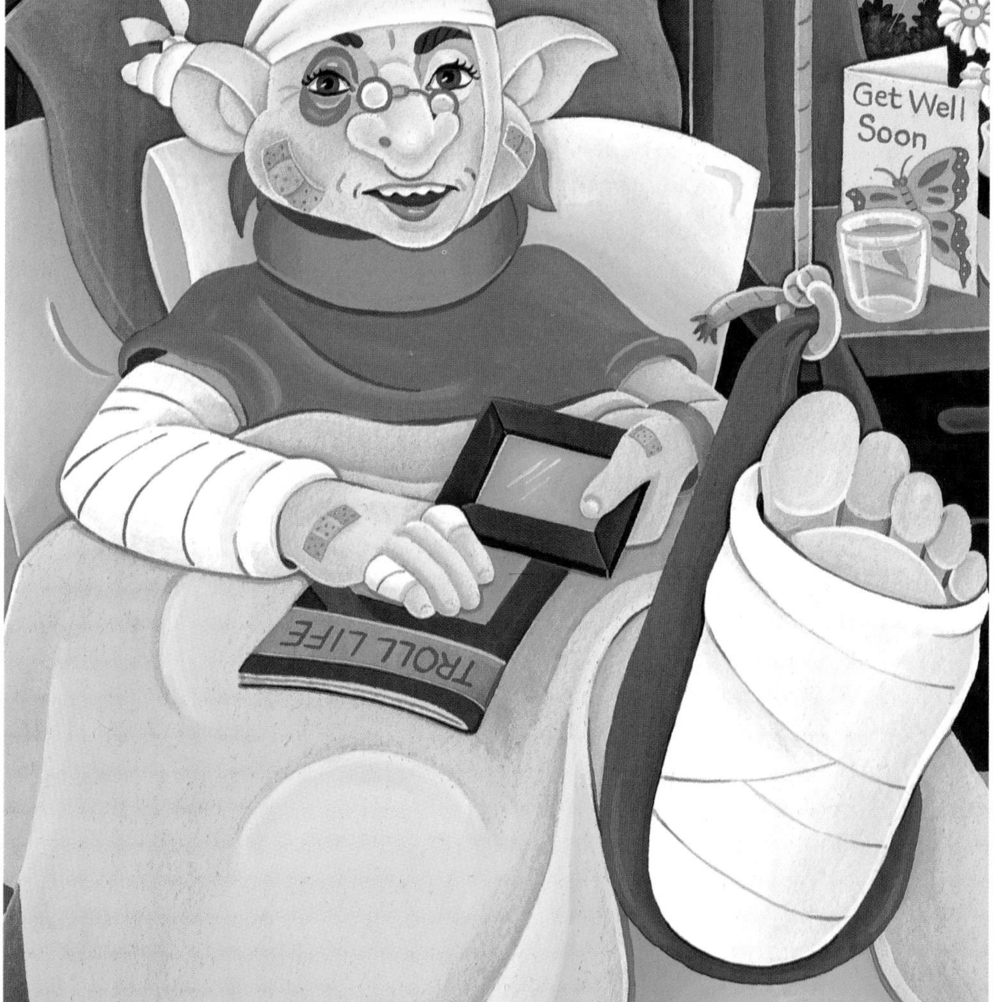

2

Just look at my face! Would you guess that I was once a handsome troll? I'm black and blue all over. And who knows how many broken bones I have? Why, I have aches on top of pains and pains on top of aches! There's not a spot on my body that doesn't ache or pain!

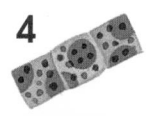

The doctor at the emergency room couldn't believe her pretty troll eyes. "I've never seen so many aches and pains on any troll before!" Her red eyes grew as big as saucers.

"What happened?" she asked. "Did a building collapse on your head? Or was it a speeding train that hit you?"

4

"Can you believe that a goat did this to me?" I asked. "I'm lucky to be alive!"

Why did that goat beat me up? He doesn't understand hospitality, that's why! It just doesn't pay to be friendly to a goat. Let me tell you what happened.

5

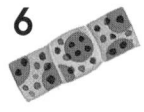

I live under a bridge not too far from here. Whenever folks cross over my bridge, I always say hello and offer them a cool drink.

If I have a good meal cooking, I invite them for dinner. It's what my mama taught me to do. "Be friendly to folks, and they'll be friendly to you," she would always say.

When I was just a little troll, I remember folks sitting on our porch and visiting for hours. Then Mama would bring out the treats. She was known far and wide for her homemade pies and fresh lemonade. So now that I live under the bridge, I try to make folks feel welcome there, too.

9

Well, one day Little Billy Goat Gruff came trotting over my bridge. "Hi, Little Goat," I yelled up to him. "How are you doing on this fine, sunny day?"

And he yelled down, "I'm doing fine, Mr. Troll. I'm trotting over to the hillside to eat the tall, green grass."

10

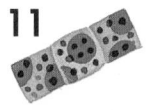

"Oh, no need to go all that way," I called
up. "I'd like to have you for dinner."

Little Billy Goat seemed scared. "Why don't
you wait for my bigger brother?" he asked.

I thought that was strange, but it was all
the same to me. I guessed that the little goat
was shy. "All right," I said. "Run along, then."
And he did.

11

At the time, I didn't know why that little
goat seemed so scared. I found out later when
the goats started wagging their tongues. They
said Little Billy Goat Gruff thought that **he**
would be dinner!

Doesn't that beat all? That little goat thought I wanted to eat him for my dinner. Where did he get such a silly idea? I guess goats aren't used to folks being friendly.

In no time at all, Middle Billy Goat Gruff came along. "Hi, Middle Billy Goat Gruff," I yelled up to him. "How are you doing on this fine, sunny day?"

14

Middle Billy Goat yelled down to me, "Hello,
Mr. Troll. I'm fine. I'm on my way over to the
hillside to eat the tall, green grass."

"Oh, no need for that," I called up. "I'd like to have you for dinner."

Again, I had no idea that the goat thought I wanted to eat **him** for my dinner. If he had only said something, I could have set him straight right away. I had a big pot of stew on the stove, cornbread in the oven, and a fresh-baked pie. I even had a big pitcher of Mama's famous lemonade to wash it all down.

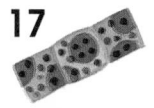

But Middle Billy Goat Gruff acted just about
the same as his little brother. He told me to
wait for his big brother.

"Well, that will be fine," I said. "You run on
along, now." I thought those poor goats must be
really shy or something. I could tell they didn't
know much about hospitality. But I couldn't have
guessed what would happen next.

In just no time at all, Big Billy Goat Gruff
came along.

"Hi, Big Billy Goat Gruff," I yelled up at him.
"How are you doing on this fine, sunny day?"

"Hello, Mr. Troll," he called down to me. "I'm
getting along fine. I'm going over to the hillside
to eat the tall, green grass."

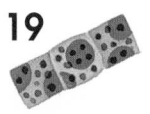

"Well, now, there's no need to do that,"
I called up. "I'd like to have you for dinner."

Big Billy Goat Gruff yelled down to me,
"Come right on up, Mr. Troll. I'll be waiting
for you!"

"Well, well, well," I laughed to myself. Finally, one of those goats was going to join me for dinner. I hopped right up onto the bridge and started toward Big Billy Goat Gruff with my hand out. Of course, you always shake hands when you meet someone.

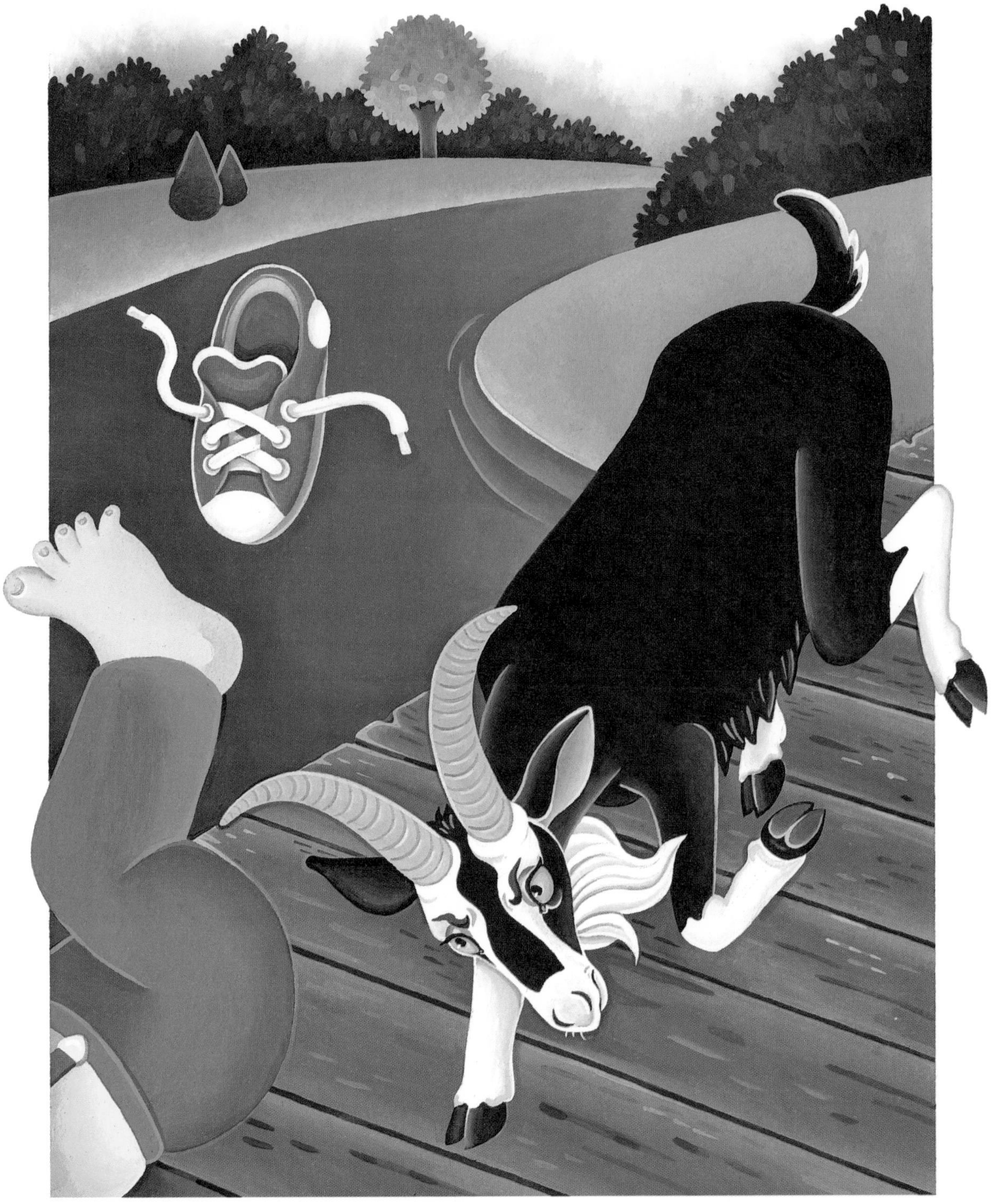

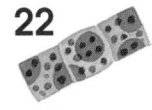

Then, from out of nowhere—

BAM! WHAM! WALLOP-A-ZOO!

Let me tell you, that goat has some big horns and hooves. He turned me every which way but loose.

"Help! Somebody save my skin!" I yelled. "This goat is out of his mind!" Finally, I dove into the water and swam down the river.

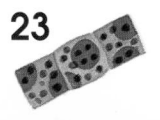

That's all I remember. I have no idea how I ended up here. I'm just lying in this hospital bed, hoping to get better. I know I'm lucky to be alive.

Next time, I'll think twice before I invite someone for dinner. And if it's a goat, I won't have to think about it even once. Goats don't understand hospitality. But I bet you do, don't you? It would be great to have you for dinner!

"I think he's going to find a new home," said Big Billy Goat Gruff.

Little Billy Goat Gruff and Middle Billy Goat Gruff smiled at one another. It sure was great to have a big brother! Then they all began to eat the tall, green grass that tasted just as yummy as it looked.

23